For Susie, James,
John and Katie
W.M.

For Violet
J.H.

Published in Great Britain by Walker Books Limited
Published by Prentice-Hall Books for Young Readers, A Division of Simon & Schuster, Inc.
1230 Avenue of the Americas, New York, NY 10020

10 9 8 7 6 5 4 3 2 1

Prentice-Hall Books for Young Readers is a trademark of Simon & Schuster, Inc.
Printed in Italy

Library of Congress Cataloging-in-Publication Data
Mayne, William, 1928–
Tibber.
Summary: After several adventures and mishaps around the barnyard, Tibber
the kitten decides to leave further exploring for another day.
[1. Cats — Fiction.   2. Farms — Fiction]   I. Heale, Jonathan, ill.   II. Title.
PZ7.M4736Ti 1986b   [E]   86-16871
ISBN 0-13-921214-0

Tibber

Written by
William Mayne

Illustrated by
Jonathan Heale

Prentice-Hall Books for Young Readers
A Division of Simon & Schuster, Inc.
New York

Tibber opens his first eye. He sees a blur.
Tibber opens his second eye. He sees a smudge.
They are his brother and his sister. Their
mother Tabby hides them in the farm stable.
Only Susie visits them and the great horses.

Their mother licks them. She sings to them. "Lie still," she says, "I'll go to catch brown barn mouse for breakfast."

"I could do that," thinks Tibber, as his mother's legs go by. "One day." But his new eyes do not see far. Tabby turns to a shadow, and she is not there.

Tibber calls for her. Smudge and Blurr call too. Dog that minds the cows hears them call, and sniffs by the door. He tips the latch, but cannot turn the lock.

Tabby comes in another way. She counts them and they learn her mousy breath.

"One day," says Tibber. He knows how brave he'll be.

"Not yet," says Tabby, and licks him head over heels, putting her paw on his squeak.

Dog rattles at the latch again, and Tabby's back goes hard and high, her fur stands out. She hisses and she spits. She slips out of the window, and attacks with scream and scratch. Dog runs off to bark at cows instead.

Tibber watches Tabby coming back. He can see farther now. Smudge and Blurr do not dare to look, but Tibber is braver than he ought to be.

"Stay in the nest," says Tabby when she goes to the farmyard to stalk a sparrow. "You're all safe in there." She goes out through the missing pane, into the bright light.

"One day soon," says Tibber. He looks over the edge of the nest, far down to the floor. He dare not jump.

"Do not be naughty," say Smudge and Blurr. "We are good, and we shall learn to wash our faces."

"I shall not even wash my feet," says Tibber. "Only kittens do such things. I shall be a total cat. One day."

Tabby drops a feather in the nest.
A sparrow has not flown home tonight.
The kittens chase the feather.

"One day," says Tibber, killing the feather
dead. "I am not afraid." But he comes to his
mother, in case he is mistaken. She licks
him and he bites her ears.

Tabby goes to the granary to get a gray rat.

"Stay at home," she says. "I'll bring your
first meat supper."

Tibber says to himself, "Today is the day. If I'm big enough for meat I'll catch my own."

He jumps down from the nest. He crosses the stable floor. He clambers to the window to see where he will go.

He goes out where the glass is missing.

"Come back," says Smudge. "Goodbye," says Blurr.

"Hello, world," says Tibber. He walks. "Come along, shadow," he says. Shadow follows, lying flat.

Dog is walking too; and Dog can eat kitten between meals. Shadow gets flatter still, and grows pale.

Tibber thinks about that very much. He thinks that Dog will not follow him up some stone steps. Dog thinks he will.

Tibber thinks Dog will not follow him up the post and then along the rail.

Dog stands on his hind legs and has a big sniff. Tibber hisses and arches his back, and falls off the rail.

Luckily it was a long way down. Tibber has escaped, all huffed and hissed, before Dog is down the steps.

Tibber runs through a doorway. He climbs along a high shelf, and jumps. He does not know where.

This place is the dairy, and Tibber is in a bowl of milk. Susie sees Dog at the dairy door and sends him off. She does not hear Tibber splash and splutter, paddling in cold milk.

Dog sits down and waits for kitten with cream.

The bowl is very full. Tibber floats to the edge. He puts a paw on it. He puts his tail on it. He puts an ear on it. He coughs and climbs out with his fur laid flat and thin.

Dog licks his lips. Tibber licks his chin. He licks his paws. They taste better than he hoped. He licks his chest, his back, his tail. He feels full, though not like total cat.

Dog has forgotten him and gone to sleep.

Tibber leaves the dairy.

He has forgotten Dog.

He is not there to share the meat that Tabby brings. She comes to find him, and to scold. Tabby sees Tibber, and dreadful Dog. She is angry and begins to shout and spit.

Dog wakes up. There is time, he thinks, to take this kitten, before he leaves.

Tibber runs, but into a corner where high walls join.

"Soon done," says Dog. "There's no way out."

But a ladder begins just there. Tibber reaches up to the first rung and stands on it. He reaches to the second, and hopes it is high enough. He balances on the third, and thinks that's all he'll manage.

Dog stands up, four rungs tall. Tibber climbs to five.

Tabby comes up behind Dog and tears him with her claws. She thinks that he will run away and Tibber will be safe.

Dog knows more than that. Dog can climb a ladder. Dog climbs. Tibber climbs, big steps for him. Dog is getting better all the way.

Tabby shouts and swears. Brown barn mice, farmyard sparrows, gray granary rats, come to see. It is like a circus.

Up goes tired Tibber, wobbly with fright.

Dog is climbing very well. Tabby is on the ladder too, and makes him hurry more.

Then there is no more ladder for Tibber. The gap at the top of the ladder is too big for him. He cannot reach the hayloft edge. He tries, but falls.

He hits the ground so hard he cannot breathe. Tabby comes to lick him and to pick him up and hurry away.

Clever Dog has climbed the ladder and is in the hayloft, pleased with himself, still looking for Tibber. He looks out and sees him, and shouts, ready to come and get him.

But that is that. Dog can climb up ladders, but has never been taught to climb down them. He is stuck at the top. He barks, quite unhappy. He dances. Rats and mice and sparrows laugh.

Susie comes. She wondered what the noise had been. She picks up Tibber, and he smells of milk. She picks up Tabby. She takes them to the nest, and strokes all four until they purr and go to sleep.

"One day," says Tibber, one eye closing, then another. "One day."

"I know," says Susie. "But not today." She goes to carry Dog down from the loft and give him his supper before dark.